KILLER IN THE TRAP

By EINAR OLSEN

Illustrations by LEE LeBLANC

published by

ODDO PUBLISHING

Mankato, Minnesota

the WONDERFUL WORLD *of* CHILDREN'S BOOKS

Advisers

Anita Bullard
Assistant Professor of English
Oswego State University College, New York

Ruth Foy
Library Coordinator
Baldwin-Whitehall Public Schools
Pittsburgh, Pennsylvania

Ivah Green
Formerly: Associate Professor of Education
Doane College, Crete, Nebraska

Rae Oetting
Minneapolis Public Schools, Minnesota

Alvin M. Westcott
Associate Professor of Elementary Education
Oswego State University College, New York

READING CONSULTANT

William E. Jones
Director of Education
D'Youville College, Buffalo, New York

TO EDUCATORS

What do you look for in a book about the sea written for young readers?

Should the story reveal the writer's life-long love and fascination for the mystery of this vast realm which some call Earth's last frontier?

Perhaps it is your desire that the writer and the artist have been able to portray accurately the true nature of the ocean world: its inhabitants, some beautiful, some grotesque; or its moods ranging from unforgettable violence to unbelievable gentleness.

Some may hope that young readers will be encouraged by what they find here to probe deeper into unknowns just for the sake of knowing, as man today probes into the dark, hidden reaches of the sea seeking to broaden his own limited understandings.

Certainly we want the book to serve as an early introduction to oceanography. We want the young reader to become familiar with an exciting area of exploration and development which offers youth a wide spectrum of intriguing and satisfying careers, and offers man some probable solutions to age-old problems.

All of these are here: feelings, information, and challenge. But these remain subservient to the real purpose, which is, to present to the young reader a story that is believable in an environment that is real.

EINAR OLSEN

The gray New England coast still slumbered when the sun rose out of the sea and bathed the tiny offshore island with warm yellow light.

Duke, the Labrador Retriever, trotted toward the peaceful harbor where bright-hued fishing boats gently tugged at their moorings.

Head held high, his short black hair glistening in the sunlight, Duke jogged across tide-worn ledges where island fishermen spread their nets to dry.

He stopped to sniff at shells and feathers and other flotsam left behind by the ebbing tide. He hurried on again as if he sensed excitement in the air.

The big dog was eager to find his friend, Splash the Seal. He moved past the cedar-shingled fishermen's shacks and stacked lobster pots.

Big Stan the Lobsterman called out from one of the anchored boats, "Come aboard, Duke." On another day the dog would have gone to watch the lobster pots being hauled, but this morning Duke only wagged his tail in reply.

From the doorway of his shack Old Herm the Fisherman hailed the dog, "Come along, Duke." Watching Herm pull in his nets was exciting, but again Duke wagged his tail and trotted on in search of Splash.

When he reached the top of the stone breakwater Duke
stopped to look ahead. Far down the rocky shoreline was
Whaleback, a huge granite rock shaped like a whale.

Island children loved to gather on Whaleback during storms to watch the gale-driven waves as they crashed upon the rocky island shore. Sometimes the onlookers were drenched by salty spray and wind-whipped spume flung high in the air by the smashing surf.

On peaceful days, Whaleback was a wonderful spot from which to fish. Old Herm's fish trap was anchored just off shore from the rock. Whaleback was where Splash the Seal was most likely to be found.

Splash and Duke were much alike. Both liked to play and swim. They understood each other's bark, and were the best of friends. Duke thought of Splash, not as a seal, but as a dog; and Splash thought Duke to be another seal. They enjoyed teasing each other, in the water and out, to the delight of the villagers and summer visitors. When Splash swam with his head out of the water as Duke did, people on shore often mistook them for two playful dogs. Duke was the faster of the two on land. His legs were long and he could run swiftly, while Splash pushed and hitched along in the clumsy style that earless seals use when moving on land.

Splash's front legs were stubby flippers, well suited for steering when he swam, but they barely supported him on land. His two back flippers were superb for swimming, but of little use out of water. Splash was so powerful a swimmer he could catch fast-swimming fish.

At times his dazzling speed protected him from enemies, but on land he was nearly defenseless. Therefore, the seal rarely went more than a few feet from the edge of water. Although Duke playfully teased his slowpoke companion on land, he also protected Splash from harm.

Much of Splash's day was spent swimming about, catching fish. He had a big appetite even if he was a harbor seal.

Harbor seals are one of the smallest seals in the ocean. Splash was about the size of Duke and had a coat of coarse yellow-brown hair covered with dark brown spots. The top of his puppy-like head was dark brown with wrinkles, giving him a puzzled look. Although no ears were visible, Splash had a keen sense of hearing.

Splash and Duke had a mutual friend. The fishermen called him Peg Leg.

Peg Leg was a black-backed sea gull of the far north. From wing-tip to wing-tip he stretched farther than a boy can reach with both arms. Peg Leg's back, tail, and wings were coal black. His head and body were snow-white. Peg Leg had a bright yellow bill and one pink webbed foot.

During a severe winter storm, the big gull had appeared in the harbor with an injured wing and one foot missing. Old Herm kept the bird in a wooden barrel in his shack and fed him fish scraps.

One of the fishermen whittled an artificial leg out of soft pine for the gull. The leg was held in place by a little leather strap which went over the bird's back. While the gull remained in Old Herm's fish shack it thumped around on the wooden leg, and the fishermen named him "Peg Leg."

When the gull was well enough to leave the shack, the wooden leg proved so unwieldy that Herm removed it. The injured wing became strong and the gull could fly again. It had no problem balancing on one foot. The bird, as if he knew that he owed his life to Herm, made the island his home. He became a familiar figure standing majestically at the bow of Old Herm's dory, looking much like the figurehead of an old clipper ship. He left the boat now and then to wheel and scream with the other gulls.

As good friends, Duke, Splash, and Peg Leg enjoyed many adventures together. To Duke, who ate but once a day, Peg Leg and Splash were constantly hungry and always hunting for fish. Peg Leg was skillful at finding fish; Splash was good at catching them. Peg Leg flew around over the harbor and out in the bay until he located a school of fish. Then he cried to alert Splash who swam out and caught enough fish for both of them. Fishing became a team effort.

As Duke came over a rise, Whaleback loomed in front of him. And sure enough, there, near the water's edge, sat Splash the Seal, eating a freshly caught mackerel. The Labrador barked a greeting; Splash barked in reply. 19

Then Splash turned seaward listening for something; Duke listened too. Far out from shore screeching sea gulls had sighted fish. One of those gulls was Peg Leg.

Dog and seal sat on Whaleback Rock looking toward Old Herm's fish trap. Dozens of raucous gulls flew over the trap. Shrieking discordantly, they dived for small fish entangled in the nets. Duke could not see Peg Leg among the others but shortly the big gull came swooping down toward them.

With a great flapping of wings, Peg Leg joined his
friends on Whaleback. They greeted each other in noisy
fashion.

Peg Leg picked up the half mackerel that Splash had been eating and swallowed it in one great gulp. Gulls can swallow a large fish in one piece. Peg Leg's strong stomach juices would soon digest his fish breakfast.

Having finished his share of the mackerel, Peg Leg was ready for more. He flapped his wings and flew out toward the spot where other gulls continued to raise a great clamor. Another school of fish had become trapped and the gulls were greedily feeding before the fishermen came to pull up the nets.

Splash, drawn by the noise and excitement, wriggled his way toward the water. He slid down the wet seaweed and began swimming away from shore.

Duke sat watching. The seal turned his head toward his friend and barked. "Come on, Duke," he seemed to be saying, "let's go fishing." The dog was anxious to join the seal but this was open ocean and Duke never had swum here before.

Duke hesitated a few moments while undecided, then cautiously picked his way down the slippery seaweed. He avoided the tiny, sharp barnacles growing on the rocks which could give him a painful scrape.

At the water's edge he crouched, then sprang into the water to join Splash. Close to shore Duke could see the colorful bottom. Long ribbons of kelp reached up to him. But soon the ocean bottom disappeared and nothing could be seen but the dark green of the sea.

Splash appeared to be in good humor this morning and began teasing Duke. The seal slid under the water, nudging the paddling dog from below. Then he explosively propelled himself into the air like a rocket, leapfrogging over Duke and falling back into the water with a mighty splash. His continual performance of this stunt in the harbor had given him the name "Splash."

Suddenly Peg Leg appeared overhead encouraging the two swimmers with a call. Old Herm's trap was teeming with fish and the gull wanted the seal and the dog to hurry. Splash swam faster. Duke paddled faster, although Splash was far in the lead. Splash could outswim almost anything in the water.

Duke and Splash followed the fish trap leader which stretched from Whaleback to the anchored trap at least 100 yards off shore. The trap leader was an underwater net fence. The top of the net was held afloat by hundreds of round cork floats. The bottom edge of the net, held down by lead weights, reached nearly to the ocean floor. The trap leader blocked the route of the schools of fish in their migration near the shoreline. Reaching the net barrier, the fish swam along the leader toward the sea, searching for an opening in the net. The confused fish swam through a V-shaped entrance into the trap — a submerged, gigantic box made of heavy fish net. It, too, was held afloat by countless cork floats and by large barrel floats at each corner. Long, tarred ropes led from the trap corners to big iron anchors on the ocean bottom. The anchors held the trap in place despite the pressures of surging tides or entrapped fish.

In the early morning, the fishermen would come in their dories, close the trap mouth, and proceed to "haul the trap." Slowly the net would be pulled into their boats until the trapped fish were herded into a special pocket at the trap's outer end. From here they could easily be removed from the trap with long-handled dip-nets.

Often Duke had watched Old Herm and the other fishermen haul the trap. It was exciting for the fishermen to look into the roily waters of the giant net from the safety of their boat and try to guess what strange sea creatures might be trapped in the net. Usually, mackerel and herring made up the bulk of the catch, but sometimes whiting, cod, sea robins, skates, squid, and even giant tuna were victims of the trap.

This morning, as Duke reached the opening of the trap, there was no clue as to what creatures might have wandered inside of it during the night. Duke paddled through the mouth of the trap to join Splash, already inside. Peg Leg maneuvered overhead, peering into the depths of the water, looking for a mackerel school he had seen earlier.

Suddenly at the far end of the trap a swirl appeared as if a giant spoon had stirred the water. Splash sped for the whirling waters which indicated a tightly packed school of fish. Nearing the spot, Splash rose in a graceful arc and plunged below the surface of the water. He surfaced, within seconds, holding a fat mackerel in his mouth. With a quick toss of his head he flipped the mackerel into the air. Peg Leg had been waiting for Splash to do this. He dived down and caught the fish in mid-air. This was a favorite stunt of the seal and the gull, and many times they had delighted tourists and the fishermen with their circus-like performance.

Duke, meanwhile, was swimming about inside the trap. He hadn't caught anything yet. The mackerel school was in a frenzy. The fish darted this way and that. Sometimes they came very close to Duke, and he lunged at them, but caught none.

Labradors are strong swimmers. Their wide feet make good paddles, and their round otter-like tails serve as effective rudders. Duke had now been in the water for a long time. He was beginning to tire.

Splash and Peg Leg had caught and eaten several juicy mackerel. Splash disappeared again, and Peg Leg, spiralling high above, watched the action. He saw Duke making unsuccessful thrusts at the passing fish.

Then from his lofty aerial view Peg Leg spotted something very alarming! A long, dark shadow appeared in the center of the trap. A gray-brown triangle shaped object was gliding along the surface. The triangular fin meant only one thing—a shark had followed the school of fish into the trap.

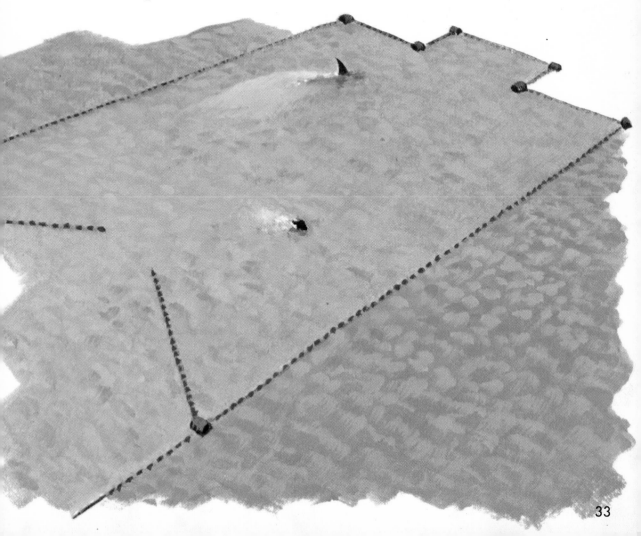

Peg Leg hovered directly over the intruder whose huge purplish-brown body was nearly as long as Old Herm's dory. Then Peg Leg saw the ugly head of a monstrous hammerhead shark. This is one of the most vicious, cold-blooded killers in the ocean. Effortlessly, the shark propelled its massive body through the water. The gull fearfully watched while the gigantic mouth opened and the shark gobbled up several fish at once.

The hammerhead's lazy twisting course was bringing it nearer and nearer to Duke who unsuspectingly kept swimming about, still snapping at the leaping mackerel. Again the shark circled. Its head moved from side to side, its piercing eyes searching the dark water. The cavernous mouth opened wide and rows of sharp teeth closed on other fish. Duke was in terrible danger. This monster could detroy him with one bite.

Peg Leg gave out a shrill warning. Duke did not heed the call, but at the far end of the trap Splash heard the gull's frenzied distress signals and began streaking toward him. Spray flew as the seal sped across the water.

Again Peg Leg dived at Duke to warn him. This time the dog sensed the nature of the gull's actions and stopped swimming.

Slowly, ominously, the sinister stalker edged toward the startled dog. For a moment the vicious fish poised motionless in the water. Then, as if noticing for the first time the presence of new prey, the ruthless killer moved forward. Terrified, Duke saw the shark approaching. With a pitiful yelp Duke turned to escape.

From above, Peg Leg must have sensed that Duke was doomed. The courageous gull dived at the shark's head in a final effort to distract the savage rush, but the killer would not be headed off. Now only a few yards separated the shark from the panic-stricken dog.

Suddenly, out of the water, inches in front of the charging shark, catapulted Splash. Into the air he rose and back into the water he fell, creating such a commotion that the hammerhead slowed for the smallest instant. Once again the brave seal came up from deep under the water and erupted into the air in front of the confused shark. This time the shark swerved and slashed at his tormenter, the seal.

That was all the time Duke needed. He clawed at the cork line; then with a mighty fear-evoked effort Duke pulled himself across to safety. He paddled swiftly for the shore. But what of his friends, Peg Leg and Splash?

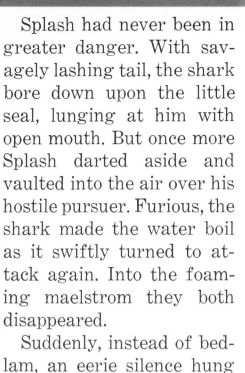

Splash had never been in greater danger. With savagely lashing tail, the shark bore down upon the little seal, lunging at him with open mouth. But once more Splash darted aside and vaulted into the air over his hostile pursuer. Furious, the shark made the water boil as it swiftly turned to attack again. Into the foaming maelstrom they both disappeared.

Suddenly, instead of bedlam, an eerie silence hung over the dark water. Peg Leg could see nothing in the inscrutable darkness of the sea. Perhaps the one-sided battle was over.

But no! In a moment, Splash broke to the surface. With quick, frenzied leaps he hurtled toward a corner of the trap. Only inches behind, torpedo-like, stormed the shark. The nets rocked with the violence of its propulsion. Again the evil mouth opened and with a desperate lightning thrust the shark lunged forward. The razor teeth snapped shut with wild fury and again a geyser of water sprayed high into the air. Out of the foam, and over the net leaped Splash. Once more his remarkable speed had saved his life.

Never had there been such a wild uproar in Old Herm's trap. The bay thundered with the great threshings and gyrations of the monster fish gone berserk. The waters within the trap boiled like a gigantic cauldron. But the violence was to no avail for the shark. His writhing and flailing only bound him more securely in the net. For him there was no escape. The din gradually subsided and finally only the mewing of the gulls along the shore could be heard.

Splash caught up with Duke, and together they scrambled up on Whaleback where Peg Leg joined them. The three adventurers, weary and still frightened, huddled together in the early morning sun. How safe and friendly their granite rock felt to them!

They watched Old Herm and the other fishermen row out in the dory to haul the trap. Excited talk followed as the men caught sight of the helpless shark, hanging enmeshed in the trap corner where the wily Splash had lured it.

"Good thing no one got in his way," exclaimed Old Herm. "That critter was a man-killer."

Herm noticed the tired adventurers on Whaleback and called, "Lucky that you clowns weren't out here this morning. You'd have been in a peck of trouble."

Duke, Splash, and Peg Leg could not answer. But had they been able to, what a tale they could have told!

about the author

Einar Olsen, born and raised on Cape Ann, Massachusetts, developed an early and lasting acquaintanceship with the sea and with the fishermen of Gloucester. As the son of a fishing captain, he was able to spend out-of-school time in quest of halibut and swordfish aboard his father's vessel, one of the last of the famous Gloucester schooners.

Following World War II Navy service, and graduate study at the University of Maine and Boston University, he entered the teaching profession. Dr. Olsen taught in colleges in Texas, New Mexico, and Minnesota before returning to Maine as a college administrator. His hobbies of sailing, scuba-diving, and marine photography keep him in touch with the sea he loves.

Olsen and LeBlanc have collaborated on four Oddo Publishing books: KILLER IN THE TRAP, THE LOBSTER KING, ADRIFT ON A RAFT, and MYSTERY AT SALVAGE ROCK.

about the illustrator

Lee Le Blanc was born in Powers, Michigan. Soon after graduating from Iron River High School he moved to Los Angeles to study art. After one year he went East and over a period of four years attended art schools in New York and Philadelphia.

Between the years 1937 and 1939, Lee did much free-lance work to improve his various techniques. In 1939 he started his Hollywood motion picture career as animator for Looney Tunes and Merrie Melodies. In 1941 he joined Twentieth Century

Fox as an artist in the Special Photographic Effects Department. In 1956 Lee became administrative head of the Metro-Goldwyn-Mayer Special Photographic Effects Department until his retirement in 1962. In 1963 he and his family, Lucille and Patricia, returned to Michigan and *personally* built their home on Brule Lake. In 1963 he was commissioned by Brown and Bigelow to create calendar subjects yearly.

In 1967 he was appointed Art Director for Oddo Publishing and has illustrated LITTLE FROG LEARNS TO SING, HORNY, WHERE IS DUCKLING THREE?, and is completing a series of elementary oceanographic titles — KILLER IN THE TRAP, LOBSTER KING, ADRIFT ON A RAFT, and MYSTERY AT SALVAGE ROCK.

In addition to art, he studies animal life closely and during the winter months he and his family help feed and care for the various species which abound on his property.